Little Library Mouse

Even when you are little,
you can imagine big.

Written by Stephanie Lisa Tara & Illustrated by Alex Walton

I'm alone . . .
I pause
The clock goes tick-tock,
My library darkens
Is that the key in the lock?

I'm skipping!
I'm sliding!
Turn a page, step inside,
Books wait like miracles
Now come along for the ride!

I'm a king
I'm a queen
Upon words I stand tall,
Paws on my scepter
I command one and all.

I'm a clown
I'm a juggler
The story pulls me in,
Applause fills my ears
Above the noise and the din.

I'm a ladybug
On a leaf
With poems to tell,
The rhyme makes me sway
On ripples that swell.

I'm a train
I'm a plane
I'm a ship in this tale,
Tip my hat in the air
On a sentence I sail.

I'm a gift
I'm a wish
On the pages I flip,
I find glossy good cheer
In this storybook trip.

I'm winter
I'm snow
Spin a silvery fable,
Frosted wilderness-white
On the library table.

I'm red
I'm yellow
I'm iridescent blue,
Short stories are rainbows
Of sharp color and hue.

I'm a lion
I'm a tiger
I discover as I read,
The paragraphs show me
What animals need.

I'm a cobbler
I am leather
I'm an elegant shoe,
Now recite in old verse
For that's what I do.

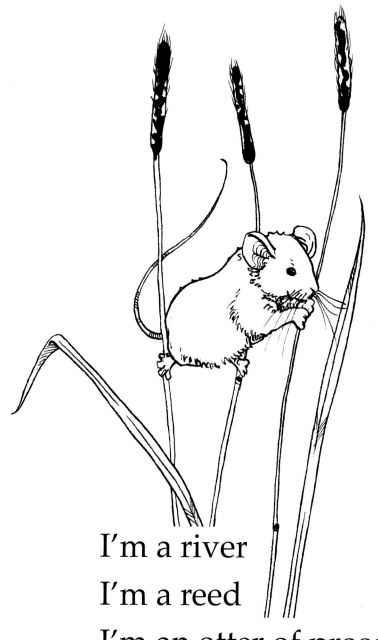

I'm a river
I'm a reed
I'm an otter of prose,
Building castles of images
For splendid new shows.

I'm a chef
I'm a cake
In a book just for cooks,
Cherries, like words
Are delicious as hooks.

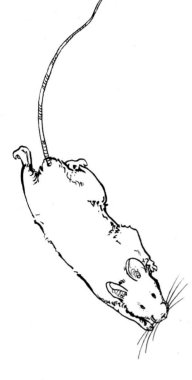

I'm the fog
I'm a secret
In a mystery plot,
I grin slyly at clues
Till I find the jackpot.

I'm paper!
I'm ink!
I've become any book,
I read, I imagine
So can you, take a look!

Dedication

~For Phil Saltonstall~
whose creative spirit inspires dreams

Little Library Mouse

For information, please contact:
Brown Books Publishing Group
16200 North Dallas Parkway, Suite 170
Dallas, Texas 75248
www.brownbooks.com
972-381-0009
A New Era in Publishing™

Hardbound ISBN: 1-933285-39-7
LCCN 2005910668
1 2 3 4 5 6 7 8 9 10